Groundwood Books / House of Anansi Press
groundwoodbooks.com

We acknowledge for their financial support of our publishing
program the Canada Council for the Arts, the Ontario Arts
Council and the Government of Canada.

 Canada Council **Conseil des Arts**
for the Arts **du Canada**

 ONTARIO ARTS COUNCIL
CONSEIL DES ARTS DE L'ONTARIO
an Ontario government agency
un organisme du gouvernement de l'Ontario

With the participation of the Government of Canada | **Canadä**
Avec la participation du gouvernement du Canada

Library and Archives Canada Cataloguing in Publication
Gay, Marie-Louise, author, illustrator
Mustafa / Marie-Louise Gay.
ISBN 978-1-77306-138-2 (hardcover)
I. Title.
PS8563.A868M88 2018   jC813'.54   C2017-907487-3

The illustrations were done in watercolor, ink, colored pencil,
water-soluble art wax crayon, soft pastel, HB and 6B pencil
and collage.

Design by Michael Solomon
Printed and bound in Malaysia

Mustafa

Marie-Louise Gay

GROUNDWOOD BOOKS   HOUSE OF ANANSI PRESS   TORONTO   BERKELEY

for Sheila Barry

Mustafa and his family traveled a very, very long way
to get to their new country.

Some nights, Mustafa dreams about the country he used to live in.
Dreams full of smoke and fire and loud noises. He wakes up.
"Where am I?" he asks.
"You are here," says his mama. She hugs him tightly.
They go out to look at the moon and the stars.
"Is that the same moon as in our old country?" asks Mustafa.
"Yes," answers his mama, "the very same moon."
Only then can Mustafa go back to bed.

Mustafa looks down at the park. It is so green.
In his country, the trees were gray with dust and dry as sticks.
He sees birds hiding in the trees.
Red birds, blue birds, yellow birds.
He sees two small animals jumping from branch to branch.
Their bushy tails wave and curl in the air. They chatter like monkeys.
"Do you want to play in the park?" asks his mother.
"Yes," says Mustafa. He runs downstairs.

Mustafa walks under the trees.

The air smells green and cool.

He sees flowers shaped like his grandmother's pink teacups.

He sees flowers that look like dragon tongues.

He finds two treasures — a white snail shell and a yellow heart-shaped leaf.

Mustafa sees a parade of ants carrying tiny blades of grass, like flags.

They look like the ants in his old country.

So do the soft, fuzzy caterpillars. So do the buzzzzzing bees.

Mustafa hears a noise. He hides behind a tree.
A girl walks in the park. She holds a ribbon tied to a cat.
In Mustafa's country, cats were skinny and wild.
They lived in the streets. They didn't wear ribbons.
The girl sees him. She says something.
Mustafa doesn't understand her words. He pretends to tie his shoe.
Then he runs back to the apartment.

"Back already?" asks his mother. "What did you see in the park?"
Mustafa tells her about the flowers that look like Grandmama's pink teacups.
He tells her about the parade of ants waving their flags.
He shows her his white snail shell and his yellow heart-shaped leaf.
"Lovely!" says his mother.
But he doesn't tell her about the girl-with-the-cat.

The next day, Mustafa sees shiny red bugs with
black spots. They look like jewels.
He finds more treasures – an acorn, a speckled stone
and a perfect drawing stick.
Mustafa draws an airplane in the sand.
He draws the house he used to live in.
He draws clouds of smoke and fire.
He draws broken trees.

Suddenly, the girl-with-the-cat is there.
She points to the drawings and says something.
Her words float in the air and disappear.
Mustafa drops his stick and runs away.
The girl draws flowers, butterflies and stars. She draws her cat.
The clouds of smoke and fire disappear. So do the broken trees.

Mustafa goes to the park every day.
The trees have turned bright orange and red.
"Is this magic?" he wonders.
He sees an old lady feeding breadcrumbs
to a whirlwind of pigeons.
In Mustafa's country, there was not enough food
to share with the birds.
The old lady speaks to them.
She must be the magician!
Mustafa wishes he could speak bird language.

Mustafa sees a small vampire chasing a fairy, a fox and a rabbit.
They are screaming and laughing.
Mustafa waves to them.
They don't see him. They disappear into the trees.

Mustafa hears music.
It winds its way through the trees like a river.
A man is playing a red accordion.
Mustafa knows this tune. His uncle Amir played it all the time.
Everyone smiles and waves and claps their hands.
A dog barks. Birds sing.
Mustafa whistles along with the music.
But nobody notices him.

"Mama," asks Mustafa, "am I invisible?"
"If you were invisible, I couldn't hug you, could I?" answers his mama.

The next day, Mustafa sees the girl-with-the-cat.
Before she can see him, he scrambles up to the top of a huge tree.
Now he really is invisible.
But the girl-with-the-cat finds him.
She makes a sign with her hand. It means "come with me."

He follows the girl to a pond filled with dark water.
The girl points. Three fat orange fish are swimming in circles.
The girl takes some yellow grains out of her pocket
and throws them into the water.

The fish rush to the surface to eat.
They make funny fish faces.
Mustafa laughs. So does the girl.

The girl leads Mustafa to another part of the park where there are swings.
She ties her cat to a tree. She sits on a swing.
The girl swings back and forth. Higher and higher. She looks down at Mustafa.
He sits on a swing. He swings slowly back and forth. Then, higher and higher.

Together, they almost reach the treetops.
Together, they almost touch the clouds.

The girl points to herself and says something.
It sounds like *"Ma-ri-a."*
It also sounds like music. Happy music.
Then she points to Mustafa.
He understands.
"Mus-ta-fa," he says.
Maria smiles.
Mustafa doesn't feel invisible anymore.

Maria

Mustafa